D0443294

APR 1 1

HELEN HALL LIBRARY
City of League City
100 W. Walker
League City, TX 77573-3899

The Slumber Party Payback

Other *RUBY* books
by Derrick Barnes

Brand-new School, Brave New Ruby
Trivia Queen, 3rd Grade Supreme

The Slumber Party
Payback

by Derrick Barnes
illustrated by Vanessa Brantley Newton

DISCARD
Helen Hall Library
League City, TX 77573-3899

SCHOLASTIC INC.

New York   Toronto   London   Auckland   Sydney
Mexico City   New Delhi   Hong Kong   Buenos Aires

If you purchased this book without a cover, you should be aware that this book is stolen property. It was reported as "unsold and destroyed" to the publisher, and neither the author nor the publisher has received any payment for this "stripped book."

No part of this publication may be reproduced, stored in a retrieval system, or transmitted in any form or by any means, electronic, mechanical, photocopying, recording, or otherwise, without written permission of the publisher. For information regarding permission, write to Scholastic Inc., Attention: Permissions Department, 557 Broadway, New York, NY 10012.

ISBN-13: 978-0-545-01762-6   ISBN-10: 0-545-01762-9

Text copyright © 2008 by Derrick Barnes
Illustrations copyright © 2008 by Scholastic Inc.

All rights reserved. Published by Scholastic Inc.

SCHOLASTIC, LITTLE APPLE, and associated logos are trademarks and/or registered trademarks of Scholastic Inc.

Library of Congress Cataloging-in-Publication Data Available

12 11 10 9 8 7 6 5 4 3   9 10 11 12 13/0

Printed in the U.S.A.   40
First printing, October 2008

To Naeemal: You know what it's like putting big brothers in check.

—D.B.

To the Brantley, Curry, Garrett, Jean, Key, and Newton Clans. For the future of Zoe, Ben, Chyna, and Isabel.

—Auntie V.

⭐ Chapters ⭐

Here's the deal: I'll be hosting my second big sleepover. Hopefully, this one won't be a disaster like the last time. My fingers and toes are extra-double crossed. If everything goes smoothly and everyone invited shows up, I'll be known at school as the girl who throws the best slumber parties in town. All I want is a party with no toads or yucky stuff in the swimming pool. Is that too much for a girl to ask?

— rb

❀⋆❀⋆1❀⋆❀⋆
Toads and Vinegar

No matter how many times I try to forget, I just can't. It seems like only yesterday. . . .

This June, I hosted my very first sleepover. It was the second day of summer. My daddy had just put a new swimming pool in the backyard for us. All of my friends, all seven of the girls I invited, seemed to show up at the same time: Teresa Petticoat, my best friend; Mona Sweetroll; Claudia, Sarafina, and Toots, three girls from

my old school; and the Piccolo twins from up the block.

Daddy had burgers and hot dogs on the grill. My big brother Marcellus was the DJ. Also, almost all of the girls were drooling over him . . . as usual. Another (and sweetest) big brother, Tyner, was helping Ma fill up the cooler with peach, grape, and mango sodas.

Everybody was having a great time, but there was something wrong. Things were going *too-too-too* well. All of my friends were about to get into the pool when I heard Teresa scream, "GOODNESS ALIVE! TOADS! SLIMY, SNOT-COVERED TOADS!!!" And that was the beginning of the end.

I looked down. A million toads started hopping out of the grass and onto our patio. Yuck! They were every color of green that girls don't like, from dried-up booger all the way to funky foot fungus.

Daddy was doing everything he could to run the toads back into the grass, but more kept coming. Ma and

Ty jumped on one of the picnic tables. Marcellus helped Daddy.

The toads had pushed me and my friends closer to the pool. We all plunked into the water with a big splash to escape the gross little green monsters. The toads couldn't leap high enough to get into the pool.

I thought everything was fine until I looked over at my friends. Everybody had turned the color of a tennis ball. Their hair and skin were bright yellow-green. I looked down at myself and I was green, too!

"Ruby, what is this? What's wrong with your pool water, girl?!!" Mona

Sweetroll yelled. At first I didn't know. When we jumped in, it was clear. All of a sudden, we were floating in what looked like a pool full of lemonade. Then I remembered that stuff called Pool Prank that you buy at the party store. It's a harmless juice that people put in their pools to play tricks on swimmers. It washes off after you get out of the pool, but it's still a mean trick. I started screaming then. I could put up with some stinky old toads, but yellow-green hair? That was too much for me to handle.

"Daddy, Daddy, is it okay for us to get out? Are the toads all gone?" I cried.

"It's fine, Ruby. You girls will be okay," my daddy said while he helped us out of the pool one at a time. He sprayed us clean with the hose, then he ran the toads out of our backyard with the hose water. "Someone put Pool Prank in the water," Daddy said.

All the toads seemed to have disappeared. Ma and Ty hopped down off the table. I looked over at my friends. They were mad, they were crying, and they were not having fun anymore.

Something told me to look up at the house, so I did. Standing in his bedroom window was my other, *other* big brother, Roosevelt. He likes to call himself Ro Rowdy. It should be Ro Rotten, because I knew he had something to do with this mess.

He looked down at me with a mean smile and waved. He had the look of a villain on his face. Then he held up his other hand and used his dirty fingers to count down from five.

Five . . . four . . . three . . . two . . . one.

At the number one, the sprinklers in the backyard came on. Just like that. All of my friends were running around and screaming. The worst part of it all was that the sprinklers weren't spouting water. They were spraying *vinegar*!

I don't know how Ro made that happen. What I wondered the most as I stood there smelling like a great big yucky Easter egg was why Ro had done this to me.

2
Okay, Let's Try
This Again

My teacher, Miss Fuqua, called out to me. "Ruby Booker! Ruby Booker! I think you dropped this. Put it in your pocket or in your fancy guitar book bag, superstar." I was running out to after-lunch recess. School had started again.

Miss Fuqua handed over one of my special slumber-party-sleepover-jam invitations. I'd made them myself. Ma had mailed them on Monday, and I'd brought extras to school. I was hoping everyone would come. Who could say no? Who in their right mind wouldn't like *my* invites?

Ruby's Slumber-Party-Sleepover-Jam
Friday, September 6, 5 p.m. —
Saturday, September 7, 10 a.m.
5388 Chill Brook Avenue
RSVP by September 4
Your Fabulous Hostess:
Ruby Marigold Booker
Can't wait to see you all!

"Hey there, girlie. I got mine yesterday," my best friend, Teresa Petticoat, bubbled. She was peeking over my shoulder. I finished reading the invite and slid it in my sock. The yellow sock, not the red one.

"My ma gave an invite to your ma on Monday, Teresa. How come you're just now reading it on Wednesday?" I asked.

"You know how things just slip my mind, Ruby," Teresa said. "Besides, it doesn't matter. You know I'm going to be there. I wouldn't miss your slumber party for the world."

"I hope everybody else feels that way. Remember the last slumber party, when Ro played those mean jokes on us? What a mess," I said.

"That was months ago. I don't even

think any of the girls remember what Ro did. At least I hope not." Teresa shrugged.

"Don't remember? I still have nightmares about my last sleepover."

"Me, too," Teresa said quietly. Then she asked, "So why are you having another one?"

"You know me, T. I'm not going to let one bad time keep me down. Ro, or a snowstorm, or even a backyard full of toads couldn't stop me," I said.

"I have to admit, Ruby, I shiver every time I think about those toads. You know how much *all* animals make my skin crawl."

"I sure do. Remember when we had that lady from the zoo bring those orangutans to school?"

Teresa nodded fast. "Girl, I could not come out from under the desk."

"Don't worry, T. There will be no orangutans at my next slumber party."

Teresa looked relieved. "Have any of the girls from our old school answered your invite?" she asked. "How about the Piccolo twins?"

"Nope. I haven't heard from any of the girls who came to the last party," I said. "Actually, the twins haven't spoken to me since the last sleepover."

Teresa looped me by the arm and led me to the jungle gym, where the fourth- and fifth-grade girls hang out during recess. "Don't worry, Ruby," Teresa said. "I know you invited Toya Tribbles and Iris Solo, two of the really nice and *really* popular fifth-grade girls. Let's ask them now if they'll be coming."

"I don't know, T. Maybe we should just wait and see if they say anything about my party." I pulled away from Teresa. I didn't want to be turned down by a bunch of older girls, especially to my face.

"Come on, Ruby. It couldn't hurt to

ask." Teresa started pulling at me again.

When Teresa and I walked over to where the big girls were hanging out, Toya and Iris were there. They live up the block from us. We have known each other for what feels

like forever. Toya Tribbles goes to our church, and Iris Solo gets dance lessons from my ma.

Toya came up to us first. "Hey, girl. Cute socks," she said.

"Thanks, Toya." Most of the time when people say something nice about my outfit I say something nice back. It's only right. "Your top is cute, too. You know purple is one of my favorite colors."

Iris came over and said, "Hey, y'all. Ruby, are you coming to dance practice tomorrow with your ma?"

"I don't know. Maybe I'll be there. You know I'm not a good dancer," I

said. Teresa nudged me. She wanted me to stop stalling and just ask them about the invites. "What I was really wondering was if you guys got the slumber party invites my ma sent out."

Toya looked away. Then Iris looked down at her cute pink sneakers. Finally, Toya said, "Look Ruby, we like you. You know that, girl. But I don't think we'll be coming."

"Why not?! It's going to be fun. You won't forget it," I said. I couldn't believe they were turning me down!

Iris said, "Well, we heard just how *fun* your parties are. Your brother Ro made sure of that."

"How'd you know about that? It's going to be different this time. Promise." I really wanted them to come.

"I don't know about you, but I don't

like frogs, I hate the smell of vinegar, and they tell me that some of those girls still have that yellow-green stuff in their hair." Iris rolled her eyes.

"Toads," I mumbled. I was starting to bubble over with anger.

"What?" Toya remarked.

"They were toads, not frogs!" I grabbed Teresa's arm and stormed away. I wasn't really mad at Toya and Iris. I guess it was Ro who had me steaming.

"So what are you going to do now, Ruby?" Teresa asked.

"I don't know. It looks like it's going to be just you and me, T," I grumbled.

"You're not acting like the Ruby Booker I know," Teresa said, waving a finger at me. "Ruby, if you have any more of those invites on you, we could pass some of them out. Your party's two whole days away. Plus, there's still Mona Sweetroll."

"Oh, yeah! I almost forgot about Mona. I haven't heard from her at all," I said. Recently, Mona and her family moved off the block to another town, where she goes to a different school. It hasn't been the same ever since she left Bellow Rock. Mona is so funny and cool. I sure miss her! I wish I could call Mona on the phone, but it's long distance, and that costs money. Daddy reminds me of this every time I pick up the phone and start to dial Mona's number. To make it worse, Mona has no e-mail address. "There's always the old-fashioned way," Daddy says. "Letters."

I hope and pray Mona got the invite I mailed with a letter begging her to come.

"So what do you say about passing out the rest of those invites?" Teresa asked.

I thought about it for a minute. The people I wanted to invite hadn't answered yet. Asking girls to come to my party now, only two days away, would look like I couldn't get anyone to come. But the truth was, I *couldn't* get anyone to come, and I really wanted to have a good party!

I ran over to my guitar-shaped book bag, which hung on the fence, and pulled out the rest of the invites.

We asked two girls from our third-grade class. First, there was Sammie Wingtips. We caught her right before she went down the slide. She looked at my invite and giggled like somebody was tickling her feet. Then she said, "I don't think so, Ruby Booker. I heard you can catch warts if a frog rubs up against you. And your parties have frogs!"

"Toads, not frogs!" I squawked.

"Well, put Sammie down as a big fat no," Teresa said.

Next, there was Cleo Washington. I knew she was going to say yes. She was new to our third-grade class, and she probably hadn't heard about the disaster at my last party.

I tried to get Cleo excited about my sleepover. "So, how 'bout it, Cleo? It's gonna be the jam. You won't want to miss it, girl."

She took the invitation, then handed it back and said, "I think we're going out of town this weekend."

I didn't believe her. She looked

like she was trying to back out of the party like Sammie did. So I asked her, "Where are you and your family going, Cleo?"

"Uhhhh . . . to the moon," she said quickly. "Yeah, the moon. My daddy works for the space company, and we're going to be the f-f-first . . ." She stumbled over her words. I knew she wasn't telling the truth.

I stopped her so that she wouldn't have to make up anything else. "You know what — that's okay, Cleo. Have a good time on the moon." I guess she didn't want to hurt my feelings. Teresa and I walked away with our heads down.

Cleo yelled out behind us, "Vinegar breaks me out in hives, Ruby. Plus, I have enough troubles at home with *my* two brothers. I hope you understand."

I didn't even turn around, but I sure did understand. Ro is always messing stuff up for me. That's what he's really good at. Making me miserable. We didn't even ask anyone else. I thought they would probably turn me down, too.

"Cheer up, girl," Teresa said. "It won't be that bad. If Mona says yes, it'll be us hanging out again like old times. The Chill Brook Three." Teresa smiled.

A sleepover with only three people is not really a slumber party. It's just two people spending the night at your house. If Mona came all the way from Wallace Park, the sleepover would be special. But I hadn't heard a thing from Mona.

✿ ★ ✿ ★ 3 ✿ ★ ✿ ★
Are You Surprised?

Well, it was finally Friday, the day of my sleepover. Teresa and I were waiting by the fence after school. Daddy was going to pick us up and take us somewhere before we went home to begin my sad and sorry party.

"Ruby, I have never seen such a droopy face before. Maybe on my grandpa's bloodhound, but I think you might even have him beat," Teresa joked.

"I'm sorry, T. This was supposed to

be the thing that would make me popular," I told her.

"Well, to me, Ruby Booker, you're always a star," Teresa said cheerfully. She's so nice. I guess that's why I love her so much. "Even though it'll be just you and me at the party, we're going to have more fun than a whole heap of sleepovers rolled into one."

"Girl, you always know what to say."

All of a sudden, my daddy pulled up in his van and honked the horn three times. He always does that. It means "Let's get a move on."

"Come on, Daddy. I can't wait to get my party started," I said with a big jumbo-jet smile on my face.

"Well, look at you," Daddy said. "This morning, you were all down in the dumps. Now you're grinning from ear to ear. That's what I like to see!"

"Mr. Booker, I'm excited about the party, too," Teresa said. "Ruby told me you have some surprises for us. So whatcha got?" Teresa folded her arms.

"It's a surprise you two won't believe," Daddy said as he leaned out of the van window.

"Try me," I told him.

"Okay, girls. Cover your eyes," Daddy said.

Teresa and I stood on the curb with our hands over our eyes. Suddenly, I heard the van door unlock automatically. It does that when Daddy pushes one of those little buttons in the front. Then I heard Daddy say, "Okay, look!"

When we put our hands down we couldn't believe what we saw. It was Mona Sweetroll!

"Who's gonna give me a hug first?" Mona said. She stood in front of the door rolling her eyes for a second and then opened her arms super-wide. Teresa and I gave her a big group hug, just like old times.

"Hey, Mona. It's so good to see you. How is it living over in Wallace Park?" I asked her.

"Don't you know I love it? Can you believe it reminds me of Bellow Rock?" she said. That's what's so cool about Mona. She says things in a question.

Plus, her braids are always neat, and she likes cute clothes, just like I do. We shared clothes all the time when she lived on the block.

Teresa giggled. "I know we're going to have a good time now."

"Don't we always have a good time when we're together? What's going to change that?" Mona said.

"NOTHING! The Chill Brook Three are back together again!" Teresa and I said at the same time.

"Come on, ladies. Let's move on to our next surprise," Daddy said. We all hopped into the van and headed out.

I wasn't sure what the next surprise was going to be, but I didn't really care.

I was with my girls, and that's all that mattered.

We rolled down Chill Brook Avenue singing "Sweet Tooth," a song from the new Crazy Cutie Crew CD. Things were just like old times. Mona sang the loudest. Teresa sang out of key. I sang the best. But together, we sounded just as good as the Crew.

"Those chocolate chips
Are calling me.
Those lollipops
Won't leave me alone.
Those candy apples

Are calling me.
Corn Crispy Treats
Won't leave me alone.
My teeth are hurting me so,
but I
JUST CAN'T SAY NO!"

We passed our house and then turned onto Fifty-fourth Street. On the corner was my daddy's store, The Booker Box. We pulled in to the parking lot, and Daddy turned off the van.

"What are we doing here, Daddy? I know you're not going to put us to work," I told him. He laughed.

"As a matter of fact, the store is closed," Daddy said before he pushed the button to let us out of the van. We got out and walked toward the building.

"Closed? The store is never closed on Friday. We need to go in and check this out, Daddy," I said.

"I guess we should. This is your second surprise," Daddy announced.

Teresa led the way. "Let's stop stalling. I say we go in and check it out, Mr. Booker."

The Booker Box sells TVs, stereos, CDs, DVDs, and video games. When Daddy opened the door, it was as quiet as church when we all have to bow our heads.

"I guess he was right, Ruby. Sure is closed," Teresa whispered.

"It's closed *down*," Daddy said as he inched over to the light switch, "all for you guys!" When he flipped the big switch on the wall behind the cash register, all the lights came on. There was a big banner that read:

THE BOOKER BOX

PRESENTS

Ruby's PRE-Slumber-Party-
Sleepover-Jam

Video Games — Music — Snacks

There was also a table full of mangoes, cantaloupe, and grapes, my favorite fruits. I saw a platter of cheese crackers, strawberry cupcakes, and little sandwiches. And to top things off, there were two big pitchers of fruit punch.

"All of this for us, Mr. Booker?" Mona asked. We just stood there in the middle of the store with our mouths wide open. The three of us were shocked out of our shoes.

"Daddy, I can't believe you shut the whole store down just for us! Thank you, thank you, thank you!" I screamed, and jumped into Daddy's arms.

"That's not all," Daddy said. "You know how we have the weekly Booker Box video game contests and you never get a chance to jump in because it's always so crowded?" Daddy asked me.

"Yeah," Mona said for me. I looked at her and giggled.

"Well, look over there. This afternoon, you girls can play any game you want." Daddy pointed to the video game section. He had hooked up video game systems to three big-screen TVs. Each of us had a game to ourselves.

"I bet my brothers, the almighty

Booker boys, would be jealous," I said to Mona and Teresa.

"Especially that rascal Roosevelt. He thinks he's the ultimate gamer," Teresa chimed in.

"Please! Don't mention his name. I want this sleepover to be perfect," I preached, with my hands up in the air. I guess I was waving off any bad ideas or pranks that Ro might send our way.

After all the snacks were gone and we'd finished playing video games, Daddy had another surprise for us.

"Before we leave, I'll let each of you girls pick a DVD that you'd like to watch tonight. You even get to keep the movie for yourself," Daddy added.

"Wow, thanks kindly, Mr. Booker!" Teresa cheered. We ran to the DVD section to grab the movie of our choice.

"I know which one I'm *not* getting," I said while pointing to a scary movie called *The Nightmares of Keisha, Bad Dreams 3*.

"I don't even want to look at the cover," Teresa whimpered, covering her eyes. "I hear that some girl saw *The Nightmares of Keisha, Bad Dreams 2*, and couldn't sleep for a month."

We picked our movies and ran toward the door. Daddy turned off the lights and then locked the doors. If the rest of the sleepover was as great as the pre-sleepover was, I could hardly wait. We jumped into the van again and headed home, ready to have more fun. On the way, Teresa and I told Mona about the other girls we tried to invite to the sleepover. All she said was, "The Chill Brook Three make the best sleepover in town."

Ro-proof Fun

"**H**ey, Ma!" I greeted my mother at the front door with a big hug and kiss. My brothers were right behind her. They had just returned from the grocery store. I had asked Ma to pick up special ingredients for the dinner that the girls and I were going to make.

"Hey, baby. Are your guests here?" Ma asked.

"Yeah. They're upstairs putting away their bags."

Ro threw his three cents in

even though nobody asked him. "What guests?" he wanted to know. "Everybody turned Ruby down for her party. I wonder why?" Ro had a smirk on his face.

One of my other brothers, Marcellus, said, "Forget him, ladybug. We got all the stuff you asked for." Marcellus carried the biggest grocery sack. Even my brother Tyner carried a sack. Ro was empty-handed. He was too busy playing with his handheld video game.

Tyner nudged me in my side. "Hey, Rube, did she come?" he whispered.

"She, who?" I whispered back, and I smiled a little. I knew who he was talking about, but I wanted to hear him say it.

"You know . . . Mona. Is she here?" he asked softly. He didn't want Ro or Marcellus to hear because they would've made fun of him. Ty has the biggest crush on Mona Sweetroll. His crush is the size of Jupiter, times ten. He was all jittery for Mona.

Ro puckered his lips toward Tyner. "Who are you talking about, Ty? Mona Sweetroll? Your sweetheart?" he said.

"He can't help it . . . he's in *looooove*," Marcellus joked as he pinched Tyner's chubby cheeks. Ro and Marcellus laughed and jabbed

Tyner. I've never seen Tyner's honey-brown face turn so apple-red.

Ma came to Ty's rescue. "That's enough, everybody." She wrapped her arms around Ty to protect him from Marcellus and Ro. Then Ma said, "Go upstairs and check on your friends, Ruby. Your brothers and I have something to talk about. Give us about five minutes."

"Okay, Ma. Can we start making our dinner when you're done?"

"Sure, baby," Ma said to me. I ran to the steps, but I didn't go all the way up. I went just far enough so Ma and the boys couldn't see me. I balled

myself up like a little roly-poly bug and listened.

"All right, boys, pay attention, especially you, Roosevelt. Tonight is Ruby's night. Period," Ma declared. I liked the sound of that. "So unless you're called on to help, to play a game, or just to be around, stay out of her space. You hear me?" Ma asked.

"Yes, Ma." They all spoke at the same time. Ro's voice was the quietest. I could tell he only half agreed.

"You don't have to worry about me, Ma," Marcellus said. "I've got my recital tomorrow afternoon, remember?"

"You know I wouldn't forget, baby," Ma said. Marcellus plays this big tall guitar-looking thing called an upright. It's a bass cello. He's good at it, too, just like with everything he does.

Ty was happy to help, but not by

staying away from us girls. "Ma, I'm always here if you need me." He giggled. Ty will say anything to be close to Mona.

"I know, sugar. If I need you for anything, I'll call you." Ma giggled back.

All of a sudden, Mona and Teresa came crawling on their hands and knees behind me. "Girl, what are you doing?" Mona said softly.

"Ruby, you know I can't sleep in your room with that critter in there," Teresa whispered in my ear. She was talking about my pet iguana, Lady Love.

When we got downstairs, Ro and Marcellus were putting the groceries away in the kitchen. Ty stayed behind with Ma. This was his chance to see Mona.

"You girls are back together again!" Ma said. "Hi, Teresa. Hi, Mona." Ma gave both of them a hug.

"Hi ya, Mrs. Booker. That dress sure is pretty," Teresa said.

"How long has it been, Mrs. Booker? Have you missed me?" Mona asked.

"Sure have. This block hasn't been the same without Mona Sweetroll." Ma smiled and winked at me. She knows that Mona likes to hear stuff like that.

While we were talking, Ty stood there staring at Mona. He wiped his sweaty hands on his shirt.

"Tyner, what's wrong with you, cutie?" Mona said playfully. Tyner is usually so smart and always has the answer to everything. But things change when Mona comes around. He stutters and stammers. It is sooooo funny.

"Who, m-m-m-me? I'm doing f-f-f-fine. How are you, M-M-M-M . . ." Tyner just couldn't get her name out of his mouth.

"Have you forgotten my name, Ty?" Mona said, winking at him.

"I didn't for-for-for-forget you. N-n-n-never." Ty shoved his hands in his pockets. Then he rocked back and forth on his heels.

"Well, Ty, excuse us, baby. This is a girl party, and the girls and I are going to the kitchen to make our very own

pizzas," Ma said. "Maybe we'll call you down for a taste."

Mona could put worms and tree moss on her pizza, and Ty would say it was the best. Poor lovesick boy.

Ty went upstairs to watch TV, and we went into the kitchen.

"I'll show you how to make a pizza pie, girlie," Teresa said to Mona. We were all wearing colorful aprons and floppy chef hats, even Ma.

We got to choose our own toppings. Ma went first. "What do you think about my pepperoni, sausage, chicken, pineapple, super-cheesy combo?" she asked us.

"Sounds good to me," I said. "But I don't think any of you will be able to hang with my veggie pizza."

"I know you can't be serious, girl," Teresa smirked. She looked at me like I was joking, but I wasn't.

"What's a pizza without a load of meat?" Mona asked. She wiped her hands on her pink apron and grabbed a handful of pepperoni.

"You don't know what you're missing," I told them. "I've got mushrooms, green and red peppers, onions, eggplant, spinach, tomatoes, and my favorite soy cheese. Man, that's good!"

"Both of you are lost in the dark,"

Teresa chimed in. Her apron was covered with all kinds of stuff that I'd never seen on a pizza.

"Do you know what you're doing?" I asked.

"You all may make pizza your own way in Bellow Rock, but in Memphis, where I was born, this is how they do it," Teresa said with her hands on her hips. "First, we have the turnip greens, ham-hock slices, black-eyed peas, corn-bread crumbs, rib-tip chunks, and then we top it all off with the best barbecue sauce in the world. Now, *that's* good eatin'." Mona, Ma, and I laughed so hard at Teresa's Memphis pizza.

When we finished topping our pies, Ma said, "Okay, ladies. Let's put your pizzas in the oven."

"What can we do while we wait?" Mona asked.

"Let's decorate and paint our toenails in different colors while we are waiting for the pizzas to be ready," Ma suggested.

"Oh, yeah! Sounds good to me, Ma," I cheered.

"Let's do it!" Teresa shouted.

"Mrs. Booker, do you know how cool you are?" Mona said as she wrapped her arms around Ma.

We went into the den, where Ma painted our toenails and put cucumber slices on our eyes. We sat back in three fluffy chairs. We looked like superstars at a spa.

Mona leaned over to me. "Ruby, do you know how happy I am that none of those other girls showed up?"

"Yeah, me, too." I said.

"I feel the very same way, guys," Teresa added.

I took the cucumber slices off my eyes and held hands with my two best friends. It felt so good being together again.

Inside, I kept hoping that we could get through the night without any stupid Ro Rowdy pranks. So far, everything was going well.

5
Oh, the Horror!

"So, what do you think, Tyner?" Mona asked my brother while he took a sharklike bite out of the extra-meaty pizza she'd made. Ty chewed and gulped really, really hard. I could tell he didn't like the pizza. But Ty is so nice, he wouldn't hurt anybody's feelings.

"It's—it's—it's okay." I could tell Ty was not being totally honest. Mona's pizza looked tough and rubbery, but Ty went ahead and ate it, anyway.

"This amazing Southern-girl pizza is really delicious!" Marcellus had grabbed a slice of Teresa's pizza. "Is that smoked neck bones and mustard greens I taste? I love it!" He gobbled that slice so fast.

We all sat at the kitchen table with Ma, Ty, and Marcellus. Daddy was in his home office, and Ro was in my room getting my pet iguana, Lady Love, to put in the basement.

"Well, Ma, since you've tasted all three of our pizzas, which one is the best?" I asked. Teresa and Mona leaned in to hear Ma's answer.

Ma tapped her long fingernails on the table and then said, "You know what, if I had to pick one . . . I wouldn't."

"Awwwwww!" all three of us moaned. I knew she was going to say that.

"I can't pick a favorite. They're all so good and all so different. You ladies did a great job," Ma said. Ma's kind of like Ty. She doesn't like to hurt people's feelings. But I know she liked my pizza the best. I just knew it by the way she smiled when she ate it.

"So what's next?" Mona asked. "What kind of fun are we gonna have now?"

"I guess we could put on a DVD. We could watch *The Chicken Nugget Princess*," I suggested. "But first let's put on our pajamas."

Teresa came up with a super-fun

idea. "Sounds good to me. I love that princess! And we can play dress up and put on our own fashion show."

"You girls can raid my closet," Ma offered. "I'll even let you try on some of my jewelry."

"Do you know how awesome that sounds?" Mona added.

We all snatched a piece of each other's pizza and zoomed upstairs with our movie.

"I tell you, Ruby, every time I come over here, your room gets cuter and cuter." Teresa always says that when she comes over.

"T, you were just over yesterday. My room hasn't changed." I giggled.

"I know, but I always notice something new in here. I swear I do."

Mona hadn't seen my room in a while. She hit me with a clump of questions. "Can you believe this dresser? Girl, where did you get that Crazy Cutie Crew bedspread?

Don't you know I love your room, too?"

Teresa stuck the disc in the DVD player. "I'll put in *The Chicken Nugget Princess*. I've been meaning to ask my mama to get this movie."

Mona turned off my bedroom lights. I shut and locked my bedroom door. I didn't want Ro to come in my room and try any of his stunts.

"Are you going to push PLAY or what?" Mona asked me.

I was trying to get comfortable first. "I want to see this as much as you do. Hold your horses," I said. Then I pushed the PLAY button on the remote control. Mona chucked a pillow at me.

"PILLOW FIIIIIGHT!" Teresa yelled out. Pillows were flying everywhere. I ducked under the side of my bed. Then I ran toward the big basket of stuffed animals that I'd put together for the girls. It was covered with a big, heavy blanket.

"I *know* you're not going for those teddy bears, are you?" Mona challenged me. She and Teresa had the same idea. When I grabbed my cuddly giraffe to throw at Mona, it felt wet and squishy. And it smelled like toe jam and vinegar!

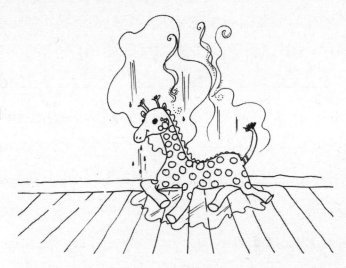

"Gross, Ruby. All of these things smell hog-bad." Teresa covered her nose with both hands. The entire basket was wet and musty.

"What is that smell?" Mona asked. I could barely hear her because she had a pillow over her nose and mouth. The smell was starting to make us sick.

I didn't want to believe that Ro was pranking us again. Especially since Ma had talked to him.

I went over to open my window, but it was stuck. Then Teresa came up to me and tapped me on the arm and said, "Uh, Ruby, I don't think that's *The Chicken Nugget Princess*." She pointed at the TV.

On the screen in big red letters was *The Nightmares of Keisha, Bad Dreams 3*. That was the horror movie none of us wanted to see! It was a scary movie made for kids, but a scary movie is a scary movie.

"Maaaaaa!" I screamed.

"Turn on the lights! Turn on the lights!" Teresa ran around the room like a scared mouse.

I flipped the light switch on the wall, but the light wouldn't come on. I ran over to the lamp next to my bed. There was no bulb. I even unplugged the TV and the DVD player, but they wouldn't go off.

"Turn it off, please, Ruby!" Teresa started to cry. She dove into her sleeping bag and covered her head. "I don't want to have nightmares!"

It was dark and smelly, and the walls were closing in on us.

Mona and I grabbed Teresa, and

we ran to the door. I tried to unlock it, but it wouldn't open. We were trapped with the funky toe-jam–vinegar smell and *The Nightmares of Keisha, Bad Dreams 3*.

"Help! Help!" We all yelled and banged on the door. I kept turning the knob, but it wouldn't open. I didn't know what to do.

"Ruby, Teresa, Mona, what's going on in there?" I heard Marcellus yell through the door.

"I'll go get Ma. Hold on!" Ty hollered.

"Help, Marcellus! Help us!" I screamed as the room got darker,

and *Keisha, Bad Dreams 3* screamed out in horror.

Ma made it to my door and said, "Girls, on the count of three, I want you to push really hard, okay? One, two, PUSH!"

When they pulled and we pushed, the door flew open. Teresa, Mona, and I rocketed into the arms of Ma and the boys. All of us fell on the floor in the hallway, smelling like bad goat feet.

"Man. You girls, you need to wash, and I mean right now," Marcellus said. He covered his nose with his shirt and then walked back to his room to practice for his recital.

All of a sudden, the fear I felt from being locked in my room turned into red-hot anger. I knew who was responsible for the bad smell and the scary movie.

"How did all of this happen?" Ma asked us.

"I'll tell you how it happened, Ma. Come with me." I stomped down the hallway toward Ty and Ro's room.

Ma, the girls, and Ty followed me. I was going to bust Ro. I knew he wasn't in his room.

"Where are you going, Rube?" Ty asked me.

"To show Ma that Ro is —" I was saying as I opened the door to their room. To my surprise, Ro was sitting at his desk, studying. On a Friday night! I knew something was up.

"What's going on, ladies? I hope you're having fun. Hi, Ma. Hi, Ty." Ro looked up and gave us a sparkling smile. I wasn't falling for it.

"Where's the glue? Where's the smelly stuff you put on my toys? How did you make that scary movie come on my TV? Where are the goods, Ro?!" I stormed around his room looking for anything I could find to prove that he was up to his old ways. But I didn't find a thing. Not one thing.

"What's wrong with her, Ma? What

is she talking about?" Ro asked like he really didn't know what was going on. Then he said, "Ruby, go back to having fun with your girls. I'm trying to study for a big test on Monday. Do you mind?"

Ma looked carefully around the room, but she didn't see anything, either. She took Mona and Teresa down the hallway so they could clean up and get ready to play dress up. Ty went to Marcellus's room. I could hear the upright bass songs floating down the hallway.

I walked toward the door. But before I left Ro's room, I said to him, "Stop it, okay? Don't ruin my second sleepover! It's not funny, so just stop it."

He turned around slowly and whispered, "What?" and made a face like he had no idea what I was talking about.

"I'm warning you. Leave us alone!" I shouted before I ran out of his room. I slammed the door so hard the walls shook. I could hear him laughing that mean and nasty laugh all the way down the hallway.

I just couldn't understand why Ro enjoyed making me miserable.

✿★✿★6✿★✿★
The Last Straw

"I don't know about you girls, but I'm going to try on that fancy green jacket and those darling brown shoes," Teresa said as we stormed Ma's closet.

"Take your time, girls," Ma called out while she arranged the jewelry. "I like what you junior divas are putting on. You girls look too fierce."

It had been almost thirty minutes since we busted up in Ro's room. I wasn't so mad anymore. Plus, the stinky smell was gone. My sleepover

had started out fun, and I wanted it to keep going. One bad prank by Ro wasn't going to stop me and my girls.

"Would I look amazing in this lovely feather hat, or like a movie star in this pretty pink scarf?" Mona stared at herself in Ma's big mirror.

"Mona, you look good in anything, girl," I said.

"Ruby, you sure know how to put these clothes on the right way," Teresa said. I modeled for them and pranced around like the star I am.

"On my feet I have sparkly ruby red slippers. This beautiful brown dress was made in Italy. The raspberry beret,

Paris. And this unforgettable smile, right here in Bellow Rock. And don't you forget it."

Mona and Teresa pretended they had cameras. They flashed and flicked a gazillion shots of me on the runway.

"Come here and try on a matching

necklace and bracelet set of your choice," Ma announced.

We swayed over to Ma's jewelry box in our fancy outfits. Mona had on a pair of sunglasses. She really thought she was a superstar.

"I'll take the green-stone-looking set, Ma. You know I love that one," I said, pointing at the necklace and bracelet.

"They're called emeralds, baby. Try them on." Ma put them on for me.

"Well, I'll take that shiny, smooth, brownish-gold necklace, Mrs. Booker," Teresa said, and pointed at the one she wanted.

"That, my dear, is called a tigereye stone," Ma explained. "You'll look absolutely, positively divine. A very good choice, Teresa."

"Mrs. Booker, could I please try on those black diamond-looking things? Wouldn't they look great on me?" Mona claimed the ones she wanted.

"Onyx and silver look really regal, Mona." Ma also helped Mona put on her set.

"You've just gotta take a few pictures of us with our outfits and jewelry on," I said to Ma. "I want to take the pictures to school on

Monday. We'll show everyone what they missed."

"That's an awesome idea, Ruby. Those fourth- and fifth-grade girls, especially Toya and Iris, will be begging to be at your next party," Teresa said.

I ran to my room to pick up my cute little digital camera. When I got back to Ma's room, the girls were already posing and ready to take a few pictures.

"Okay, Ruby, jump in there and give me your best billboard pose," Ma said as she got ready to snap my picture. We were so happy and were having so much fun.

"We're ready, Ma," I said while Mona, Teresa, and I posed against the room's big window.

"Instead of saying cheese, Mrs. Booker, would you mind if we said something else?" Mona asked Ma before Ma pushed the button on the camera. "Don't you think that saying cheese is so played out?"

"Whatever you say, Mona," Ma responded. Mona was right.

"How about we say Chill Brook Three?" I suggested.

"Sounds good to me," said Teresa.

"CB Three it is. On three — one, two, three," Ma counted.

"Chill Brook Three!!!" we shouted. Ma pushed the button, but nothing happened.

"What's wrong, Ma? Push it again." I kept on my picture-taking face.

"Okay. I'll push it. Uh-oh!" Ma dropped the camera. She couldn't believe what had just happened. When she pushed the button the second time, a big cloud of yellow powder shot out at us. Even though we weren't completely covered, it was just like we were with that yellow-green stuff in the pool at my first sleepover. Ro had done it again. I just knew it.

"Maaaaaa! What is this stuff?

Ah-choooo! Ah-choooo!" I couldn't stop sneezing. Teresa was sneezing, too. Mona was sneezing even more.

"Wait a minute, baby. The yellow cloud smells like baby powder." Ma ran around with tissues for us to blow our noses with.

"It's Ro who did this, Ma. I know he must have gotten one of those powder joke cameras. It's Ro. *Ah-choooo!!!* Let's go get him." I wiped my watering eyes and runny nose. Also, when I looked down at the camera, I could tell that it wasn't mine. I should have known.

We all stormed back down to Ro and Ty's room. The door was shut, but I didn't even knock. I just kicked it. When it opened, Ro was sitting on the floor, humming and polishing his church shoes. His side of the room was clean (it never is). That boy is a professional snake.

"Back again? How can I help you ladies?" he asked with that fake nice-boy voice.

"Where's the powder, chump?" I barked.

"Ruby! Don't call your brother that," Ma told me.

"Ma, you know he's at it again. Tell Daddy to lock him in his room until he's a hundred years old." I was boiling mad.

"Ruby, he's already in his room. There's no proof that he did anything wrong." Ma shrugged her shoulders. I could tell she couldn't understand how Ro was doing all of his stunts from his room. "But to be safe, you stay put, Ro."

"*Ah-ah-ah-chooooo!*" Teresa and Mona super-sneezed.

"Okay, Ma," I sniffed. "We'll head back to my room and go to bed. Good night." I put on my saddest puppy-dog face ever.

"Sweet dreams, girls," Ro said. "I'll keep an eye out for whoever did those mean things. You can count on me." He gave us a wink and a thumbs-up.

"Your daddy fixed your DVD player, removed that stinking basket, and fixed your door. Good night, girls," said Ma. We gave her back her clothes and jewelry, then we slowly dragged ourselves into my room. I shut the door and locked it.

"I can't believe your brother would do this to you again. What's his problem, girlie?" Teresa sounded so ready to go home. Ro was chasing my best friends away.

"The question isn't what's his problem, but what are you gonna do about it, Ruby?" Mona sounded like she couldn't take any more. She has brothers, too, but she's the oldest. I may be the youngest, but now Ro had gone too far.

"Good question, Mona. I prepared just the thing in case Ro pranked us again," I said, rubbing my palms together.

"So what's the plan?" Mona
questioned.

"I hope you've got something good,
and something downright wicked!"
Teresa looked at me and winked.
She wanted to fight back, and so did
Mona and I.

"As long as you girls have my back, follow my lead, and go along with my plan, we'll get him back," I explained. "He'll not only leave us alone, but he'll never ruin a sleepover again."

I went to my closet and pulled out a big bag of tricks from the top shelf. I emptied everything out onto my bed. Teresa and Mona had no idea what they were looking at, but I did.

It was the end of Roosevelt Booker's sleepover-destroying career.

❀⋆✲⋆7❀⋆✲⋆
Say Cheeeeese!

I looked at my cute orange-and-purple fake-diamond watch. "We're right on time. Ro usually washes up and brushes his teeth around nine-thirty. It's nine-twenty now."

"So what's the plan, girl?" said Mona. She was ready to do whatever I had planned.

"Teresa, I'm going to need you to go down to the boys' bathroom and swipe Roosevelt's toothpaste."

"Which one is his, and why am I taking his toothpaste?" Teresa asked.

"It's the tube with the motorcycles and whales on it, and I'll explain when you get back. Now, go!" I shoved her out the door. She tiptoed all the way down the hall and back to my room.

"You did it! Good job, Teresa." We saluted each other like we were secret spies.

"That was exciting. That was close. That was sneaky. Yay!" Teresa enjoyed her part in the plan.

"So what are you going to do with Ro's tube of toothpaste and that other one in your hand?" asked Mona.

"This toothpaste isn't really toothpaste. It's a prank I got from the party store last Halloween. It's called Chomper Cheese. It smells and tastes like toothpaste, but it turns your teeth the color of cheddar cheese for a whole week."

"I love it!" cheered Mona. "It sounds good, but can't he just wash it out?" she asked.

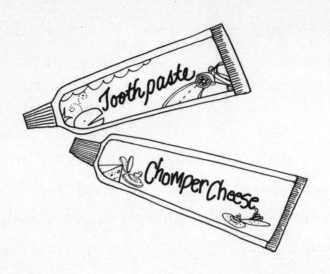

"Yes, he can wash it away, but it will take a few days to get the Chomper Cheese off of his chompers."

"Now I really love it. Let's do it." Teresa cheered.

"*Shhhh*, girl. Are you trying to give us away?" I nudged Teresa. "Since you want to be so loud, you sneak back down the hallway and put the Chomper Cheese where Ro's toothpaste was. We only have a minute left," I told Teresa.

"Okay, okay. Here I go again." She took off, tiptoeing down the hallway, but faster. As soon as she made it back to my door, Ro came slithering out of his room. We ducked back in my room and waited.

"I know his routine. He washes his face first. Then he uses mouthwash," I said, looking at my watch. "Right about now, he should be brushing his —"

"WHAT IN THE WORLD IS HAPPENING TO MY TEEEEEETH?!!"

Ro yelled like he was on fire. Everyone came running out into the hallway. Marcellus stopped practicing his upright bass and ran out of his room. Ma and Ty came from the family room. Daddy came rushing upstairs from his office.

"What's that in your mouth, Ro?" said Ty.

"It looks like you brushed your teeth with nacho cheese." Marcellus laughed, then we all did until we were rolling on the floor in the hallway.

Even Ma cracked up when she stood behind Ro in the bathroom mirror. "It'll be okay, Ro. Maybe it'll just wash out."

"I tried to wash it out, Ma, but my mouth still looks like I flossed with an orange crayon," Ro whimpered.

"Well, what happened? Where did you get that toothpaste?" said Daddy. He held back his laugh a little bit.

"I'll tell you what happened, Daddy. It was Ruby and her crazy little friends. They did it to me," Ro cried, and pointed at us.

We looked at him like we were clueless. Then Teresa said, "Whatever do you mean, Roosevelt? We were in our room doing girlie things."

"Yeah, Ro. Maybe you got one of your prank gadgets mixed up with your real toothpaste." I winked at him like he does at me. Man, that felt good.

"Well, I've got some more work to do in my office. Stop all of this hollering up here, guys," Daddy said before he rumbled back down the stairs.

"I'm going back to my room to finish practicing," Marcellus said. "Maybe I'll put on my headphones. See you later, Ro Nacho."

Ty went back downstairs with Ma. Ro stared in the mirror and gargled with anything and everything he could. The girls and I headed back to my room to plan part two of the payback.

Ro stuck his big head and cheesy teeth out of the bathroom door and said to me, "I know you did this, Ruby. Pranking is not your thing. You don't know who you're dealing with."

"And neither do you," I turned around and answered. "I've been nice for too long, but no more." Then I marched back down to the bathroom and stood right in his face and said, "You're gonna wish you'd kept your stupid little stunts to yourself when I'm through."

He gulped really hard, like he knew I meant business. "Whatever, girl. Quit playing." Then he went back inside

the bathroom, shut the door, and washed his mouth out for another twenty-five minutes.

For my next prank, I needed Ty. It's a good thing I had Mona.

✿ ⭐ ✿ ⭐ 8 ✿ ⭐ ✿ ⭐
Pretty-boy Ro

"**Y**ou want me to do *what*?" Ty couldn't believe that I was asking him to help us pull the second and biggest prank on Ro. I hated to use my sweet brother Ty, but it was time to do something useful with the crush he had on Mona. Plus, I knew that he would love to see Ro get a taste of his own medicine.

"You know what strawberry shortcake does to him, Ty. All we need you to do is take some in the room and get him to eat it," I told him.

He didn't seem to want to be a part of our plan.

"What are you gonna do to him once he's — forget it. I don't want to know." Ty refused to help me. "I don't think so, Rube. If he finds out I helped you girls, he'll be super mad and will play a trick on me." Little did Ty know that my secret weapon was about to walk through the door.

"Anybody order this?" Mona came into my room holding up two desserts like she was a waitress. They looked good, too. I made the desserts myself, but I knew that if Mona gave some to Ty, he would say yes to helping us.

"Ummm-ummm-ummm . . . I did. I mean, I love, I love, I love, straw-straw-straw . . ." Ty stuttered.

"Yeah, yeah, yeah. I know. But will you help us?" I asked as I leaned against Mona.

"Now, Tyner, are you telling me that you have to think twice about helping us poor little helpless girls?" Mona batted her long lashes and then fed Tyner one of the strawberries on a spoon.

He closed his eyes and said, "Divine and d-d-d-delicious." He chewed the strawberry like he had never had one before.

I asked him again while he was in a Mona trance, "So, Ty, are you gonna take it in there and give it to Ro? As much as he pranks you, I would think that you would really help us."

He didn't even open his eyes. He just kept chewing slowly and said, "You're right, Rube. Sure. No problem." Mona handed Ty the tray with two pieces of strawberry shortcake on it.

"As soon as you've given him the cake, lean out of the door and give us the thumbs-up, okay?" I said to Ty.

"Sure, Rube. Anything for M-M-Mona." Ty strolled out of the room and down the hallway.

"So, tell me again what strawberry shortcake does to Roosevelt? I'm just not following your plan, Ruby." Teresa said.

"Well, I don't know if it's the whipped cream, the cake, or the strawberries, but one of them knocks him out like a hibernating bear," I explained as I gathered makeup from the same prank bag where I had kept the Chomper Cheese.

"Well, why does that matter?" Mona said as she went through the different shades of lipstick I had.

"It matters because Ro has been in need of a nice makeover for a loooong time." I winked at the girls.

"Oh, no, you're not, Ruby Booker — I LOVE IT!" Teresa exclaimed. "We're gonna make Roosevelt look so pretty in pink, right?"

"You've got it. As soon as Ty gives me the signal, we'll go in and paint that snake up like a supermodel — or a superclown," I told the girls.

We eased out of my room with makeup in our hands. We tiptoed softly down the hallway like our feet were made of cotton balls. When we got to Ty and Ro's door, all three of us stuck our ears to it so we could hear what they were saying.

"Can you believe what those girls did to me?" I heard Ro say.

I had to *shush!* Teresa. She looked like she wanted to giggle, and I didn't want to get caught.

"I can't walk around with my teeth looking like this," Ro continued.

"I don't know, Ro. Maybe it was somebody else," Ty said.

"Who? Marcellus? You? You two wouldn't do that to me," Ro grumbled.

"Later for those girls — what is that you have in your hands, man?" I could hear his lips smacking. Even though he knows strawberry shortcake makes him sleepy, he just can't resist it.

"Oh, this? It's just a couple pieces of strawberry shortcake I found in the refrigerator. Want one?" Ty asked.

"You know how that stuff knocks me out, but I can't say no." Ro gave in. I heard his fork scrape a plate, and that was it. He sucked that cake up like a vacuum cleaner.

"Dang, Ro. You want mine, too?" Ty offered.

"Why not, runt. I'll take it." Ro attacked the second piece, and it was gone in seconds. He let out a big, disgusting burp! I could even hear him smacking his belly.

"Was that enough, greedy?" Ty chuckled.

"Oh, yeah. I'm good. Ro Booker's gonna sleep tonight, baby!" He sounded full and happy.

Then Ty said to Ro, "There's two more in the refrigerator. I'm going to get one. Want me to bring you another one?"

"Nah. Two was enough," Ro said.

"I'll be back," we heard Ty say as he walked toward the door. The girls and I scampered to the hallway next to Ro and Ty's bedroom.

Ty peeked around the corner, saw us, and then gave us a thumbs-up. It wouldn't be long. Ro usually falls asleep within fifteen minutes. So we waited.

After a while, Ty nudged the door open slowly and peeked in the room. And just like I thought, Ro was on the floor, snoring like a bull.

It was showtime!

"Come on, girls, let's move," I said to Teresa and Mona.

I had the pink blush, Teresa had the sparkly purple powder, and Mona had the red-hot lipstick. We propped Ro up against the side of his bed, surrounded him, and went to work.

"What are you guys doing? I didn't know you were going to put makeup on him! This is going to be so funny!" Ty laughed. I knew he would love it.

"Now, Ruby, are you sure he's not going to wake up?" Teresa wanted to know before we got started.

"Don't you hear that loud snore? Watch this." I pinched Ro's nose. I pulled his ears. He didn't move.

Mona put red lipstick on as thick and as messy as she could. "Has he ever looked as pretty as he does now?" she asked us.

"No, he hasn't!" Ty said. He was enjoying the whole thing.

Next, I put the pink blush on Ro's cheeks, chin, and forehead. He looked like he'd gotten a tan from a pink sun. I'm not good at putting on makeup, and it showed.

"Well, will you looky here. It's my turn now," Teresa said as she dabbed a sponge in the sparkly purple powder. Ro's lips looked like clown lips, his eyes were sparkly and messy. His cheeks were rosy and smeared. He looked gorgeous and ugly at the same time. I even grabbed my real camera and took a bunch of pictures of him.

We all stood up and took a good look at Ro. Then the door squeaked open, and it was Marcellus. He said, "Hey, Ro, where is my—what's going on in here?" he asked us.

"Well, we were—" I started to explain.

Marcellus just shook his head and said, "You know what? I don't even want to know. Continue." He covered his mouth so that Ma and Daddy couldn't hear him laugh and went back to his room.

Ty helped us put Ro in his bed.

I tucked him in like Ma does. We all gave Ty a high five and tiptoed to my room.

Mona turned to me and said, "Do you know, that was the most exciting, funniest thing I've ever done?"

"You think that was something?" I told her. "Wait until morning."

Then my friends and I left Ro. We went to Daddy's computer to print out the photos we'd just taken.

9
Who's Laughing Now?

"I CAN'T BELIEVE THIS! SOMEBODY, HELP! GET THIS STUFF OFF OF ME!" Ro cried from upstairs. He was the last one to wake up and the first one to see his makeover in the mirror.

It was a beautiful, sunny Saturday morning. Everybody but Ro was downstairs having a good breakfast. We girls helped Daddy make stacks and stacks of waffles topped with all sorts of fruit.

"Roosevelt! Are you okay, honey?"
Ma cried out. Ro came stomping down
the stairs, one step at a time. When he
made it to the kitchen, Ma and Daddy
couldn't believe their eyes.

"Boy, what happened to you?" Daddy
got up from the table. He went over to
Ro to get a closer look.

"Looks like he stuck his head in a bag full of firecrackers and paint," Marcellus said.

"Let me help you clean it off, baby." Ma ran over to Ro to get a closer look, too.

"Either those girls did it," Ro said as he pointed at us, "or Tyner did it. Which?"

"Ty didn't do it. That's just not his style," Marcellus jumped in.

"Well, it must have been you girls. Right, Ruby?" Ro came over to my chair and waited for me to confess. I looked up, saw his face, and laughed until my tummy started to hurt.

The lipstick was bright red, the blush was caked on his cheeks and chin, and the glittery purple powder made his face glow.

"I have no idea what you're talking about, doll face." I grinned.

"Do you think we would stoop that low, Ro?" Mona asked.

"Whoever did it, Roosevelt, they sure did make you as pretty as a peacock," Teresa chimed in before taking a forkful of her waffles.

"The one thing I'll admit," I said, "is that we have pictures of you with all that makeup on."

"Where are they?" Ro snapped.

"That's for us to know and you to find out," Teresa said. Mona just laughed and laughed.

"Ma, Daddy, are you just going to let them get away with this? I want justice!" Ro shouted. His pink cheeks flared, and his shiny red lips poked out in anger.

"First of all, you need to calm down, son. Don't come down here ruining our breakfast," Daddy told Ro, all seriouslike.

Ro turned to Ma and begged, "Please, Ma, tell Ruby to get this stuff off of my face and out of my mouth." He fell to his knees.

"Look, Roosevelt, I told you to leave those girls alone. This is the second sleepover that you tried to ruin. Don't beg me, beg Ruby." Ma turned her head and kept right on eating her waffles. "And an apology to your sister might help."

Ro looked at me with tears in his eyes. His face turned from sadness to fighting mad. Then he said, "I'm not begging you for anything, Ruby. Ro is nobody's chump." He grabbed a waffle, scooped up his skateboard, and busted out of the back door.

"He'll be back. Trust me," I told everybody.

I looked out the window, and there he was. Ro hadn't gone down to the skate park, after all. He was just sitting on the curb. I bet he was wondering what his next move was going to be. He really couldn't go anywhere with all that makeup on his face.

After a while Ro tried to wash his

face, but a lot of the makeup wouldn't come off. His lips were still a little red, and there was still some pink on his cheeks and eyeshadow on his eyes.

The girls went upstairs to pack their things. Then they stood by the door and waited for their parents to come.

Mona's dad honked his car horn. Mona gave us a hug and said, "This was the best sleepover of all time."

"The Chill Brook Three forever!" I shouted. We hugged again before she walked out the door.

Teresa's mom came next to pick her up. Teresa hugged me. "I had a wonderful time, Ruby Booker. See ya at school on Monday, girl."

I gave her a high five and watched her get into her car.

After the girls left, my whole family and I went downtown. We always go there on Saturday mornings to shop and eat lunch and to look at the tourists taking pictures of Bellow Rock.

On the way, Daddy looked at Ro in the rearview mirror and shook his head. I could tell he was trying not to laugh.

Every person we passed downtown looked at Ro. Every street vendor or owner of a fancy clothing shop we

went into with Ma stared at Ro like he was an alien from Saturn. Even after he scrubbed his face, the makeup showed.

"That poor little boy," one lady said.

"Where did they get that kid from, the circus?" a man asked his wife.

When we ate lunch at the Triple Dragon Chinese Buffet, people continued to stare at Ro's face.

Ro finished his shrimp and noodles and then sank down low in his seat.

Ma leaned over to me and said, "Honey, don't you think Ro has learned a lesson? How about apologizing? He's still your brother, baby."

As sad as I started to feel for Ro,
I wasn't going to give in. Nope, I wasn't.
I told Ma, "I want to make sure he
never messes up any of my sleepovers
again. Besides, he's never said he was
sorry for the pranks he played."

When we got back home, it was
time to get ready for Marcellus's

upright bass recital. We all got dressed up. Me and Ma wore pretty dresses and shiny shoes. Daddy and the boys wore ties.

Ty came to my room after he got dressed and said, "I can't believe Ro is still walking around with some of that stuff on his face. Not even the strongest soap can get it all off."

At the recital, Marcellus played so well. He stood up on that stage all tall and sure of himself. He plucked that bass with his fingers and hugged it real tight. At the same time, his jazz teacher, Ms. Silvernoat, played the piano while two of her other students played the drums and a shiny horn.

At one point in the recital, I heard someone sitting behind us say, "That boy looks weird."

Ro heard, too. He got up and went to the boys' room and didn't come back to his seat for the rest of the recital.

When we finally made it home, everybody was tired. While I was feeding Lady Love pieces of apple, I heard a knock at my door. It was Ro. He stood in my doorway and didn't say anything. Then he came in and plopped on my floor.

"Okay, Ruby. I give up. What do you want me to do? I'll do anything to get the rest of this girlie-goo off my face and to get my hands on those pictures you took when I was asleep," he begged. "Even though some of the makeup is off, I can't go to school like this. And I sure can't let anybody see those photos of me with all that makeup on. Help a brother out."

"You'll do anything?" I leaned in closer to look in his eyes. When he's not telling the truth, his eyes twitch. They didn't twitch this time.

"Yes. You got me. What is it?" he wanted to know.

"Okay. First, I want you to write 'I'm sorry' letters to every girl who came to my first sleepover."

"Okay, okay! Is that it?"

"Hmmph. You wish." I rolled my eyes at him. "Teresa, Mona, and I want to go to the new Crazy Cutie Crew movie on Monday. We want you to pay for it and sit with us. Mona's dad is going to make a special trip to drive Mona here."

"Come on, Ruby! All of that? You want me to spend all my allowance money on you girls?"

"That's right. You got it, brother," I said.

"You know I was going to put that money toward a new bike. Why are you fighting back now?" he said with his bright red lips all screwed up.

"I don't play, Ro," I said. "So do we have a deal?"

He looked me straight in the eye and said, "Nope. I don't think so."

I pulled out the pictures of him with fresh makeup on. "You think your boys at school will get a kick out of these pictures, Ro?"

"You're getting just as bad as I am." He couldn't believe how far I was going. "I'm angry with you. But something weird in me is kind of proud of you for sticking up for yourself." He started walking out of my room.

"So what are you going to do?" I asked him.

"I don't know. I don't have a choice, do I, Ruby?" Then he clomped down the hallway. He didn't leave his room for the rest of the weekend.

He was right. He didn't have a choice. But as Sunday came and went, I wondered who would give in first, Ro or me.

❀ ★ ❀ ★ 10 ❀ ★ ❀ ★
When a Prankster Makes Good

On Monday morning, I went downstairs before anybody woke up. Well, I thought no one was awake until I peeked in on Ro sitting at the dining room table. He'd gotten most of the makeup off his face. He was writing the apology letters, stuffing them into envelopes, and then stacking them up.

He was really doing it!

He got up from his chair with the letters and started to come in my direction. I ran upstairs to my room. Ro tapped on my door, but I didn't answer. I pretended I was asleep. Lady Love was snoring, so maybe Ro thought it was me.

He tapped softly on the door one more time, then whispered, "Ruby, here's a letter for you. I'll mail all the other letters to your friends. . . . I'm sorry."

He slid my letter underneath the door. I heard him go back to his bedroom. The letter had grape jelly stains on it. Messy, messy, messy, but I couldn't believe what he wrote:

Dear Ruby,
Sometimes I can't help myself. I

don't mean any harm. It's all in fun. Sometimes I go too far. I'll try my best to never, ever mess up any of your sleepover parties again. I'm sorry I hurt you and your friends. I guess I deserved all that makeup, but can you please get rid of those photos you and your friends took of me looking like a lipstick clown? Please, Ruby!

Meanwhile, hide this letter!

DON'T SHOW IT TO ANYONE!

(I still have a reputation to keep up.)

Your brother,

Ro Rowdy

I couldn't stop smiling after I read Ro's letter. I read it again and again and again. This was the nicest, sweetest thing Ro had ever said to me. Roosevelt Booker saying he's sorry? It would probably never happen again. I held the letter to my heart, then put it in the zipper compartment of a purple purse way up on the shelf in my closet. I got the photos of Ro in makeup off the shelf and ripped them into little pieces.

I went down to Ty and Ro's room and knocked quietly. Ro opened the door, and I could see Ty, still asleep. I didn't say a word. Ro didn't say a word. I handed him the ripped-up photos. He took the pieces and shoved

them in his pocket. Then what
happened next was a bigger surprise
than the letter.

Ro looked around to make sure
nobody was watching, then kissed me
really fast on the forehead.

* * *

Later, at school, I got another surprise.
"Ruby Booker! Ruby Booker! Put the
brakes on it, sweetie!" my teacher,
Ms. Fuqua, called out, just like she
does every single day at recess. I
hung up my guitar-shaped book bag
like I always do and looked for
Teresa. Almost every girl I passed said
hi to me.

"Hi, Ruby Booker," said a fourth-
grader I didn't know.

"Having a good day so far, Ruby?"
asked super-popular Iris Solo.

"That's my girl Ruby, right there!"
said very super-popular Toya Tribbles.

Teresa came running at me through a group of fifth-graders. "I've been looking for you, girlie. Guess what I just heard?"

"What, T? Calm down, would ya?" She was breathing heavily. I didn't know what was going on.

"Well, somehow, Mona told her cousin, who goes to our school, that we had the biggest and best sleepover in Bellow Rock. Everybody wants to come to your next party. Can you believe it?" Teresa was completely out of breath.

"Wow, T!" I said then. We gave each other our favorite double-pinky Chill

Brook Three handshake. That's when Toya Tribbles and Iris Solo came up to us.

"Hey, girls!" Toya greeted Teresa and me like we were members of the Crazy Cutie Crew.

"Hi, Toya. Hi, Iris," I said.

"Hey, Ruby. Hey, Teresa. Heard you had lots of fun this weekend." She leaned in and asked, "Is that true?"

"We sure did. Right, T?" I bumped Teresa.

"Whew, who are you telling? It was the best time I've ever had. I can't wait until the next Ruby Booker sleepover. When is it again?"

"Well, girl, I don't know. We're still making the plans. It's going to be bigger than all the others," I said. Truth was, I didn't know when I was going to have another sleepover, but Iris and Toya didn't know that.

"If it wouldn't be too much trouble, Ruby, do you think Iris and I could, you know, drop by your next party?" Toya crossed her fingers and waited for my answer. Iris did, too.

"I don't know just yet. The waiting list is already full. I'll have to get back to you girls, okay?" I nodded, hooked arms with Teresa, and walked away as cool as ever.

"Waiting list, huh? Ruby Booker, you sure are something." Teresa laughed. She was right. Ruby Booker *is* something special!

11
He's Still My Brother

"**C**ome on, Daddy. Do I have to?" Ro stood at the ticket booth begging Daddy to let him back out of his promise to me. Monday evening we all went to the movies on Sixty-third Street and Van Peebles Avenue.

"Yes, you do, son. Be a Booker of your word," Daddy told him, and then handed him his ticket to the premiere of the Crazy Cutie Crew's latest movie, *Who's Your Cutie?!?* "Your mother and I will be in theater number

ten watching *I Left My Heart in Gary, Indiana*. Tyner and Marcellus will be in theater eight watching *The Revenge of Keisha, Bad Dreams*."

"I wanted to see that. Dang, Daddy." Ro pouted. I could see Ro through the glass door. Teresa, Mona, and I were getting movie goodies, thanks to Ro's allowance money. He bought our tickets, too, just like he said he would.

"Come on, Roosevelt. We can't enjoy the Crazy Cutie Crew movie without you!" Teresa hollered out.

"*Shhhhh!* Keep it down." Ro ran over to us and covered his face. "I'm coming. I'm coming."

"Ro, who would you rather spend two long hours singing girlie songs with?" Mona asked him playfully. He just frowned and followed behind as we went into the theater.

I turned around and almost didn't recognize Ro. He'd stuck a fake hairy gray mustache on his upper lip and big dark brown sunglasses over his eyes. He didn't want any of his friends to see him.

"Do I have to sit next to you girls?" he asked.

"You know it, buddy," I said.

The lights dimmed, and then the whole theater cheered like it was a real live Crazy Cutie Crew concert. We all went nuts. Everybody but Ro was having a good time.

He was slumped down in his seat. His head was tilted to the side. He was frowning. But I couldn't enjoy the movie seeing Ro like that. He may be a prankster who gets on my nerves, but he's still my brother, and I love him.

"Excuse me. Excuse me," I said as I tried to pass Ro and my girls to go back to the snack stand.

"Where are you going, girl?" Mona shouted over the loud audience.

"Yeah, Ruby. Hurry back, ya hear?"

Teresa waved me away and never took her eyes off the screen.

I went and bought two big chocolate bars, nachos with hot peppers, a chili dog, and a large blueberry slushy. I even used *my* allowance money on everything. The lady at the stand gave me a big tray to carry all the stuff.

"You got it, baby? That tray is bigger than you are." She laughed.

Somehow, I made it back to theater six without spilling anything. Ro saw me coming into the row of seats carrying all the food. "Girl, you gonna eat all of that by yourself?"

"No way. I need your help, Ro." He took his sunglasses off, and his eyes got as wide as the movie screen. A smile found its way back to Ro's cheeks.

"You didn't have to do this, Ruby." He took the tray in his hands and tossed as many nachos with hot peppers in his mouth as he could.

I sat next to Ro. I patted him on his leg and said, "I know I didn't have to. I wanted to."

He gave me one of his smiles and then kept wolfing down his food.

Daddy always says, "At the end of the day, you're forever a Booker." And that's the truth. Even though Roosevelt can be a mean Booker boy at times, he's still my brother. I will never tell anyone about the letter he wrote me. The most important thing is that he's sorry for what he did. And now everybody can't wait for my next slumber party. Veggie pizzas, here comes Ruby!

— rb

☆ High-flying Ruby Booker soars to new heights in her next book! ☆

The plan is simple: Ruby and her BFF, Teresa Petticoat, are going to be the best flipping, dancing drill team in Bellow Rock! All they have to do is learn some moves. That's where Ruby's big brother Marcellus comes in. Even though he's not a cheerleader, he's super-fun — and Ruby is super-positive he can teach her how to flip. Then she can teach Teresa. And who knows?

Maybe this cheerleading thing will land them in the spotlight at Hope Road Academy. Read *Ruby Flips for Attention* and find out if the girls — and Marcellus — have what it takes to step up!

✭ About the Author ✭

Derrick Barnes is the author of the series Ruby and the Booker Boys: *Brand-new School, Brave New Ruby* and *Trivia Queen, 3rd Grade Supreme.* He's also written *Stop, Drop, and Chill* and *Low-down Bad Day Blues* as well as books for young adults. He is a native of Kansas City, Missouri, although he spent a good portion of his formative years in Mississippi. A graduate of Jackson State University, he has written bestselling copy for various Hallmark Cards lines and was the first African-American male staff writer for Hallmark. Derrick and his wife, Tinka, reside in Kansas City with their own version of the Booker boys — Ezra, Solomon, and Silas.

Meet the fabulous Ruby Marigold Booker!

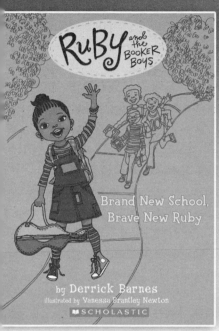

Think it's hard to stand out when you're the baby sister of the most popular boys on Chill Brook Avenue? Not for Ruby! She sings like nobody's business, has a pet iguana, and dreams of being the most famous animal doctor on the planet!

www.scholastic.com

LASTIC and associated logos
ademarks and/or registered
narks of Scholastic Inc.

A Little Sister Can Be A Big Pain—
Especially If She Has Magical Powers!

SCHOLASTIC

www.scholastic.com

SCHOLASTIC and associated logos are trademarks and/or registered trademarks of Scholastic Inc.

SISMAG